WHERE'S LARRY?

The Colouring Book

Illustrated by

Philip Barrett

THE O'BRIEN PRESS
DUBLIN

Larry the Leprechaun is on a unique and exciting tour of Ireland, visiting all the best and most famous places around the country. Even though he knows them really well, he needs your help in bringing them to life by colouring them in.

As you will know, leprechauns are special to Ireland, but they are small fellows and very hard to spot, especially in black and white. They each have a crock of gold and they hide them all over Ireland, not just at the end of rainbows! Your job is to find Larry, his crock of gold and his favourite items which are all hidden throughout this book. But you must not get on the wrong side of this leprechaun or he will make things very uncomfortable for you.

Larry has lived here a long time, he's as old as the hills! So he knows all the best places in Ireland to hide.

Can you find me and colour me in?

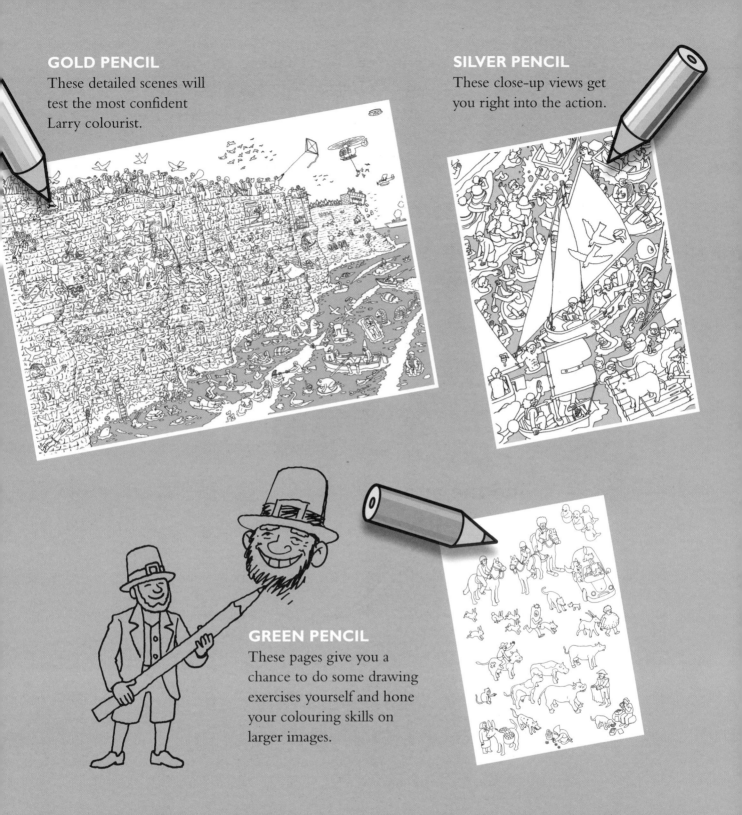

GOLD PENCIL
These detailed scenes will test the most confident Larry colourist.

SILVER PENCIL
These close-up views get you right into the action.

GREEN PENCIL
These pages give you a chance to do some drawing exercises yourself and hone your colouring skills on larger images.

See if you can find **Larry**, his **crock of gold** and his **favourite items** in each of the **Gold** and **Silver** scenes. Even if you've seen these locations in Larry's other books, Larry is hiding in a **NEW location** in each one!

Larry the Leprechaun

Larry's Crock of Gold

Larry's Favourite Items

Magic Paint Tin

Magic Paint Roller

Magic Paint Brush

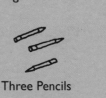

Three Pencils

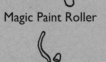
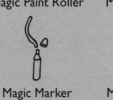

Magic Marker

Magic Spray Paint

THE CLIFFS OF MOHER A fine windy place to start our circuit of Ireland. These are the highest and steepest cliffs in the whole country. They're up to 214m high and 8km long. Don't go too near the edge! Every so often there's a HUGE wave off the coast here and surfers – really good surfers – try out their skills on it. But don't try it yourself, now! That's the Atlantic, and it is big and cold and dangerous. You're looking at America out there, you know (even if you can't actually see it). Now, can you see ME? I hope not. And, even more important, can you see me crock of gold? I'm watching you!

CLONMACNOISE This is a grand place, right beside the River Shannon where I like to fish. Monks built the monastery here hundreds of years ago and there are so many carvings around the place that it would take you all day to see them! I like the two big round towers, meself, they're perfect places for hiding!

Animal Magic
Ireland is full of all sorts of animals, from the native red squirrel to the puffins on Skellig Michael. I remember when there used to be wolves all over the place!

ST PATRICK'S DAY PARADE This is O'Connell Street, Dublin, outside the GPO on St Patrick's Day, 17 March. It's mad altogether. Them bands make a fierce racket even in this wide street – I can see why those fellas are trying to climb the Spire to get away from it (I hope they don't slip down!). The thing I don't like is the snakey thing – St Patrick drove them fellas out, you know, and here he is again trying to get rid of the very last one, it seems. Is his work never done? I'm not sure about that flying fella either – he must be able to see everything from up there. Hmm!

GALWAY BAY
My favourite regattas are the ones with the old boats. The oldest boats in Galway are called 'hookers' (I swear).

Water, water everywhere
Wherever you are in Ireland you're never too far from the water. Here's a page of water activities that give you a good chance to break out the blue pencils!

GARDA

NEWGRANGE We're really talking OLD here. This place is as old as ME! The mound was made about five thousand years ago as a burial place. And there's a great trick here: at the winter solstice in December sunlight shines through a channel into the inside of the hill and lights up a chamber there. I watched them working on all that – it took a lot of figuring out, I tell you. Now, where's me crock of gold? I hope it's not inside in that hill …

BUNRATTY CASTLE We're back in County Clare at a castle first built by the Normans. It was burned down a lot because everybody wanted to own it and they all fought over it. Now it's full of old furniture and things and I like to sneak in sometimes and have a snooze on one of those lovely beds. They're just the right size for me!

VOTE

Vehicles

I've got to know the highways and byways of Ireland pretty well on foot but every now and again I like to grab a lift.

THE NATIONAL MUSEUM Janey Mac, it's a leprechaun's dream with all the gold here – I can't decide what to look at first, there are glass cases full of bracelets and earrings, the necklaces and coins. There's even a little boat made of solid gold! It's enough to make me head spin! Just take care you don't get lost; you wouldn't like to be locked in here with the bog bodies!

BEN BULBEN That poet fella W.B. Yeats loved this mountain and I'd say it could be haunted by his ghost. Well I remember him walking up and down reciting bits of poetry while I was searching for gold. And whenever I bumped into the Celtic warriors and their huge hunting dogs I had to hide real quick.

Pastimes & Occupations
Can you colour in these characters and name what they are doing?

1.

2.

. . . .

4.

5.

6.

. . . .

8.

9.

10.

. . . .

12

13.

14.

. . . .

1. Priest 2. Golfer 3. Bodhran Player 4. Bartender 5. Irish Dancers 6. Guitar Player 7. Football Player 8. Rugby Player 9. Garda 10. Waitress 11. Angler 12. Farmer 13. Fiddle Player 14. Accordion

SKELLIG MICHAEL Watch where you're putting your feet when you climb up the steps on this rocky island – you could put your foot in a gannet's nest. Up at the top – 600 feet above the sea! – you'll find the little beehive huts built by the monks long, long ago – I remember them well, running up and down the steps in their brown robes. They weren't really men for the gold, they were more into their books. More recently, I was here, hiding in a hut, when the American film makers came to film *Star Wars* – I hope they didn't leave any aliens behind them!

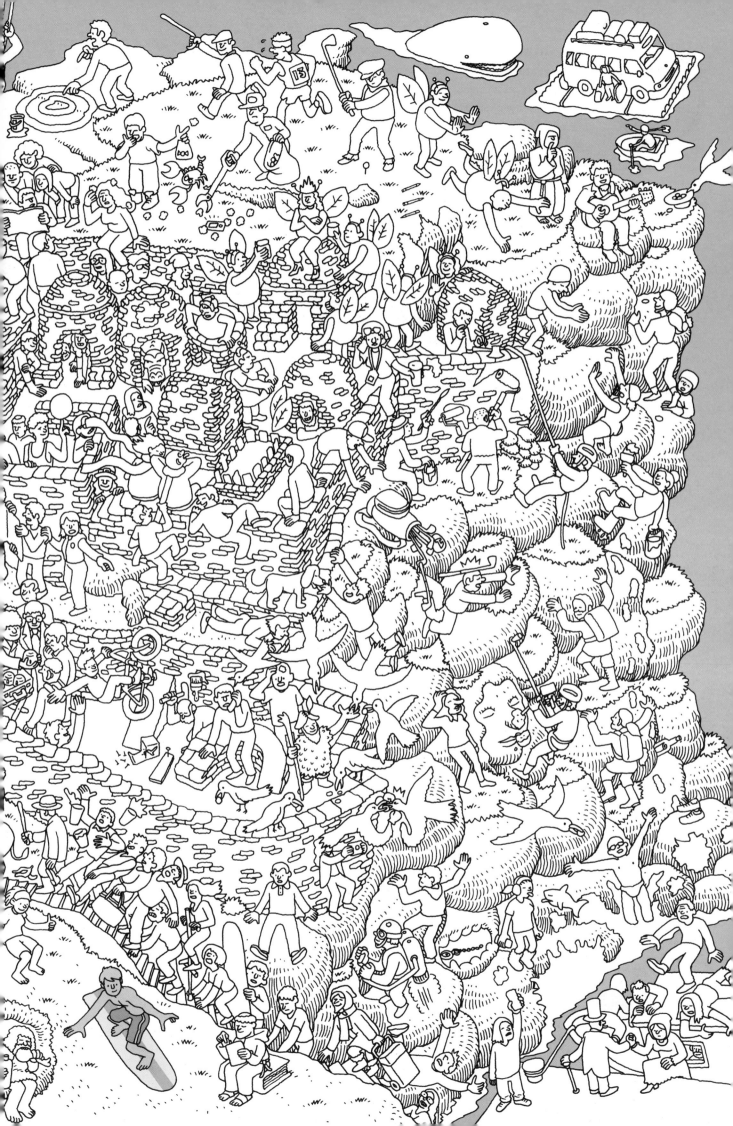

DONEGAL CASTLE This used to be the finest castle in Ireland, let me tell you, but there's no royalty living here anymore because they all left in the Flight of the Earls hundreds of years ago. They sailed out of Donegal Lough and found fame and fortune around the world. I prefer to stay in Ireland, meself, there's enough adventure for me here!

Weird & Wonderful

I've come across all sorts of folk on my travels around Ireland. Here's a page of some of the odder ones to colour in. Use your strangest colours here!

COLLEGE GREEN This is in the middle of Dublin city. There's Trinity College on the right, where you can go and see the Book of Kells. And the building on the left is the old parliament building — Ireland was (sort of) ruled from there up to 1800, when it was closed down. I remember it well — all those lords arriving on their horses to make the laws. Very grand it was. Now the place is full of noise — cars and buses driving by all the time. I'm a bit scared of it, to tell you the truth. Full of chancers too, so I've hidden me stuff and meself very carefully.

CROAGH PATRICK
This is the holiest mountain in Ireland where every July people climb to the top in memory of St Patrick himself. Some of them take their shoes off to do it! I remember this mountain from pagan times and I know all the best hiding places. Ha!

WESTPORT HOUSE I remember it when the great Granuaile – noblewoman, sea captain and clan leader – lived here. But I always stayed far away from her for fear she'd take me gold! Now, the big house is beside a beautiful lake where you can pedal around in the famous swan boats. It's much more peaceful these days, and safer for a little leprechaun!

DUBLIN CASTLE GARDEN
Did you know the name 'Dublin' comes from 'Dubh Linn' or 'Black Pool'? This garden is where that black pool used to be. I used to fish in it! Now it's a park in the middle of Dublin, a fine, private place to while away some time counting me gold. But watch out for the snakes on the paths!

Draw your own Larry

At this point you probably think you can recognise me among a crowd pretty easily. But do you know me well enough to draw me yourself? Here's how:

1. Take a pencil and lightly draw in some guideline shapes

a). Add in an oval for the head and a rectangle with rounded corners for the body.

I'm about four heads high in proportion. Did you know a fully grown human is about seven heads tall?

b). Draw in some divider lines to give the shapes volume.

c). Use lines for the arms and legs and ovals to give the rough position of my hands and feet.

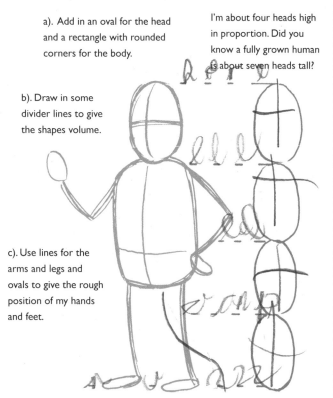

2. Using a heavier pencil or pen start to add in the lines for my clothes.

The brim of my hat starts just above the centre divider of my head.

Thicken out my arms and legs and add in the details of my clothing.

I like to tuck my trousers into my socks!

Don't forget to add in a line for the back of my coat.

3. Here's a closer look at drawing in my head and face

a). My eyes are drawn along the centre line of the head oval – I'm almost always smiling!

b). The top of my nose starts where the two head lines meet.

Why do you think I wear a belt on my hat?*

c). Don't forget the dimples of my grin!

* On a windy day it keeps my hat on

4. Now you can rub out those guidelines and tidy me up a little!

Colour me in!

Hide your own Larry

There's something missing from these two scenes – can you spot what it is? Yes that's right – good old yours truly. Now that you've learned a few things about hiding have a go at hiding **me**! And, as well as me, draw in yourself, your friends and family – whoever you want. Remember the more the merrier and the harder it will be to find me. Whatever you do don't forget to add me crock of gold!

First published 2018
by The O'Brien Press Ltd.,
12 Terenure Road East,
Dublin 6, D06 HD27, Ireland.
Tel: +353 1 4923333; Fax: +353 1 4922777
E-mail: books@obrien.ie; Website: www.obrien.ie
The O'Brien Press is a member of Publishing Ireland.

ISBN: 978-1-78849-007-8

10 9 8 7 6 5 4 3 2 1
22 21 20 19 18

Printed and bound by Gutenberg Press, Malta
The paper in this book is produced using pulp from managed forests.

Published in
DUBLIN
UNESCO
City of Literature